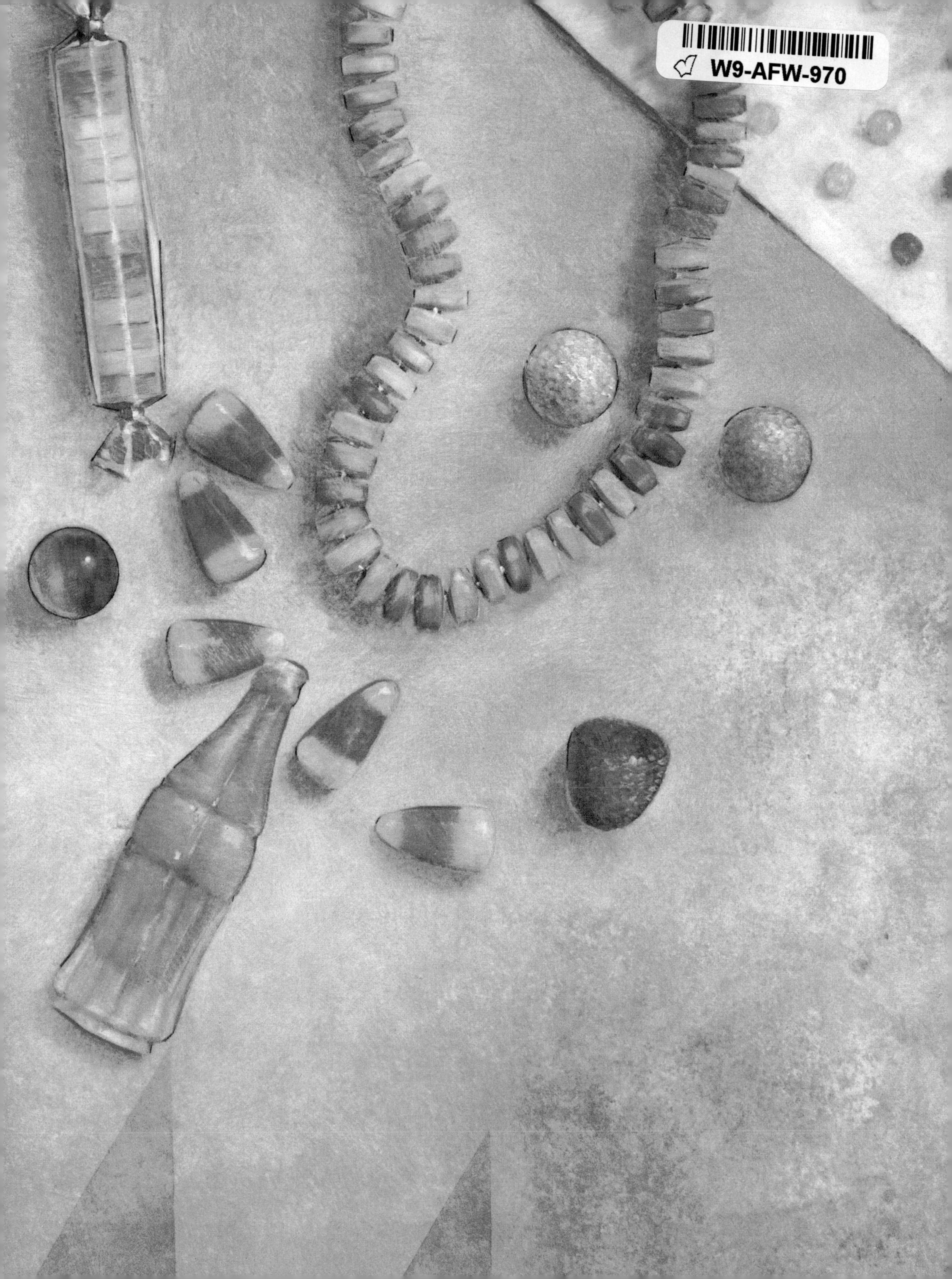

KAREN KINGSBURY

#1 BESTSELLING AUTHOR

LET'S GO ON A
MOMMY
DATE

ILLUSTRATED BY
DAN ANDREASEN

ZONDERkidz

ZONDERVAN.com/
AUTHORTRACKER
follow your favorite authors

Dedication:
To Donald, my forever love
Kelsey, my bright sunshine
Tyler, my favorite song
Sean, my smiley boy
Josh, my gentle giant
EJ, my chosen one
Austin, my miracle child
And to God Almighty, who has—for now—blessed me with these.

K. K.

For Katrina
D.A.

Let's Go on a Mommy Date
Copyright © 2008 by Karen Kingsbury
Illustrations © 2008 by Dan Andreasen

Requests for information should be addressed to:
Grand Rapids, Michigan 49530

Library of Congress Cataloging-in-Publication Data
Kingsbury, Karen.
  Let's go on a Mommy date / written by Karen Kingsbury ; illustrated by Dan Andreasen.
     p. cm.
  Summary: A mother describes several possibilities for sharing special time with her child, but finally realizes that just snuggling together and reading a book is fun and will be remembered warmly.
  ISBN-13: 978-0-310-71214-5 (jacketed hardcover)
  ISBN-10: 0-310-71214-9 (jacketed hardcover) [1. Mother and child–Fiction. 2. Stories in rhyme.] I. Andreasen, Dan, ill. II. Title. III. Title: Let us go on a Mommy date.
  PZ8.3.K6145Le 2008
  [E]–dc22
                                                      2006004528

Published in association with the literary agency of Alive Communications, Inc., 7680 Goddard Street, Suite 200, Colorado Springs, CO 80920, www.alivecommunications.com

Zonderkidz is a trademark of Zondervan.

Published in association with the literary agency of Alive Communication, Inc. 7680 Goddard Street #200, Colorado Springs, CO 80920, www.alivecommunications.com

Editors: Bruce Nuffer and Betsy Flikkema
Art direction and interior design: Laura Maitner-Mason

Illustrations used in this book were created using medium with tool.
The body text for this book is set in Bembo Regular.

Printed in China

08 09 10 11 12 • 10 9 8 7 6 5 4 3 2 1

Let's go on a Mommy Date, a time for me and you.
How about we take a trip across town to the zoo?

We'll take the path to Africa, see zebras and gazelles,
making sure the crocodiles and rhinos all are well.

We'll giggle at the monkeys,
talk to tigers, growl at bears.

We'll hunt for hippos in the
pond and lions in their lairs.

Lunch will be near tall giraffes, trick sea lions will come next,
then kangaroos, and leopards loud, and all the furry rest.

And if we get out to the zoo and find the creatures sleeping,
We'll go another day when they're all flying, climbing, creeping.
But I still want a Mommy Date before it gets too dark.
And if it's not the zoo, then maybe let's go to the park.

We'll climb up to the tippy-top, then slide from way up high.
Side by side we'll swing until our feet can touch the sky.

And then we'll play we're horsies—I'll chase you and you'll chase me.
Let's swing across the monkey bars and climb the tallest tree.

When we're finished we'll kick off our tennis shoes and socks
And race across the soft green grass, real careful of the rocks.
But if we get out to the park and rain begins to pour,
we'll have to change our special plans and have some
    fun indoors.

So what about our Mommy Date?
Hey, wait—I have a thought!
The circus would be wonderful, a rainy day or not.

We'll buy a ticket to the show and watch the circus man.
Side by side we'll laugh at clowns and elephants on cans.

Popcorn, cotton candy, and the bearded lady's smile,
with strong men lifting barbells, and the trapeze flyer's style.

Jugglers juggling fire, and we'll step right up to play
ring toss or the softball throw, we'll win a prize that way.

And if we get out to the tent and find it's taken down,
the clowns and flyers and wild tigers all have left this town,
don't be sad—our Mommy Date can happen on a farm,
where we can wear our rain boots and sip cider in a barn.

We'll watch the farmer milk a cow and maybe taste some cream.
Side by side we'll pick some veggies—you and I a team!

We'll put the corn and pumpkins in a basket at my side,
and then we'll hitch a wagon and we'll take a long hay ride.

We'll visit with the baby lambs and get a chance to pet 'em.
When evening time brings fireflies we'll chase 'em and we'll catch 'em.

And if we find that Farmer John has gone off to the beach
and closed the farm and barn up tight, his veggies out of reach,
still we'll have a Mommy Date, a place where we can go.
Say, what about the movies? We could go and see a show.

Mermaids swimming under sea or superheroes brave,
side by side we'll laugh out loud at fishies on a wave.
A story of a talking bear who laughs and likes to read.
A captured princess and the prince who saves her on his steed.
A magic tale of castles grand, a dragon breathing danger.
A little boy who's lost his dog, a brave young army ranger.

And if it's close to supper and the movies start too late,
after dinner then comes bed, I guess we'll have to wait.
So what exactly can we do just you and I right here,
to make a memory, find a smile we'll keep so very near?

Hey wait, you're here beside me now, is this our Mommy Date?
Never mind the other places. Here we are. Why wait?
One day we'll go to the park, the circus, farm, and zoo,
but for today let's cuddle with this book, just me and you.

See, time will take you far from here; you're growing way too fast.
All I want is Mommy time to make the moments last.
Something we'll remember so that come some far-off day,
you'll know how much I loved you 'cause we took the time to play.

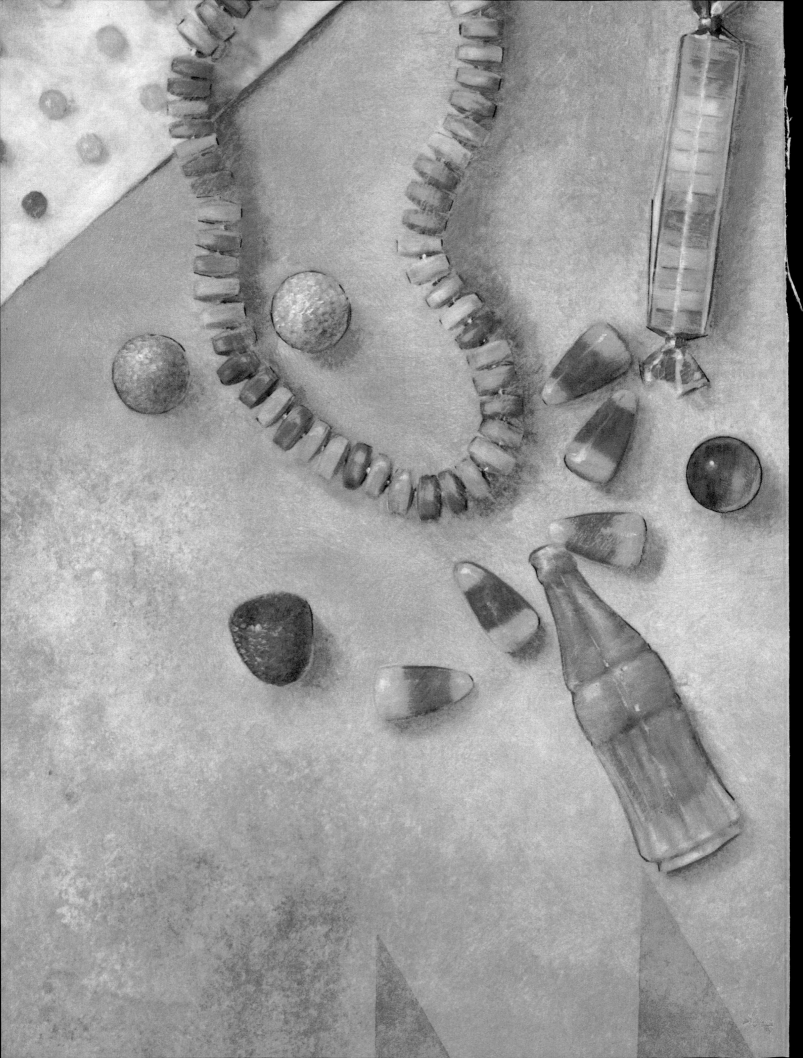